STR8 UP THUGG'N

Darrell King..............................Author

Darrell King................................CEO

Elbert   Jones

Jr.............................COO

Publisher............KJ Publications, Inc.

D1519902

Chapter 1

Located right at the intersection between the 31st Street and the 33rd Ave in Minneapolis, the Fuller's house was the only blue-roofed one in the hood. Although the blue roof didn't really fit the brown walls, it was definitely looking like a warm and friendly house. At first, it surely was a lovely place to live in. When John and Priscilla married, this house was the best thing ever, and when Priscilla got pregnant and was told she was going to have twins, they were the happiest parents ever. She gave birth to a boy and a girl, they named the boy Rupert, and the girl

Tatiana. It was all nice and sweet until one day.

It was summer, and the 6 years old twins were left home alone. Their parents went to a party, and didn't return until the next morning. During the night, Rupert and Tatiana played a lot around the house, as they couldn't sleep, and when they started to play hide and seek, and Rupert climbed in the washing machine, it was fun no more. Tatiana, being a mindless child, pushed the big button she saw her mom pushing whenever she did the laundry, thus starting the washing machine with Rupert inside. The next day they found him dead, and it was then when the nightmares begun.

Tatiana grew up as a hated child, being beaten for her brother's death whenever the chance showed up.

"He died 'cause of yo, dumb bitch!" Priscilla would yell all day long, without even thinking about the fact that Tatiana was only six when the tragedy happened. Even so, Tatiana grew up a knockout. Besides, she was witty, everyone in high school liked her, and things were only seeming to get better and better for her. She got accepted in Longfellow Alternative's cheerleading team, her high school, which was close enough to her house, and made her happier than ever. Despite her being a brilliant student, her life home didn't get easier. Her father became a drug addict, and her mum developed an alcohol dependence since the incident with Rupert. It was difficult even for Tatiana, who some viewed as a bad bitch. Her only escape was her boyfriend Seth, who loved her more than anyone.

It was late evening. Tatiana got back from her cheerleading rehearsals before the great football match between Longfellow Alternative and the South High School. It was a big event for Tatiana, so she never skipped a rehearsal. As she opened the door, she saw Priscilla laying on the floor drunk, and John violently searching through a wooden cupboard.

"Not again…" she whispered.

"Where the fuck are they!?" John snapped aggressively.

"I haven't seen them." Tatiana was sick and tired. John turned to her.

"You fucking what? Yo dumb ass dare talk to meh?!"

"I… I haven't seen them." This time she looked him in the eyes. John didn't say anything, instead she slapped her so hard she fell on the floor and you could see tears rolling down her left cheek.

"I fuckin' warned ya, I fuckin' told ya not to mess with me!" He pointed a shaking finger at her, and left. Tatiana got up and that's when she knew she had to do something about it. Her parents were tearing her apart. She called Seth.

"Seth? Where you at?"

"I'm in mah mom's car. On the parking lot. Whaddup?"

"He beat me again…" she murmured through tears. "I am afraid, Seth"

"Know wha', come'ere, you gonna sleep at mah place tonight." And so she did. She took her backpack and left snapping the door yelling how much she hates her family while leaving.

They didn't sleep that night, instead they made plans about running away.

"I have a hommie in South Carolina."

"Seth…" Tatiana wasn't sure if she wanted to do that.

"Charleston. A cool place, he says. He has a trailer no one lives in. We could be chillin' there, Tats!"

"I don't know, Seth, I wanted to go to college… I have my dreams here…"

"Know wha', yo folks are killin' ya slowly, Tats, you can't stay here forevah."

Deep inside she knew Seth was right. But she wasn't ready for something like that.

"They won't stop dissin' you, unless we run away, and ya know it!"

"We ain't got no money, Seth… we gonna starve if we go there." Seth didn't reply, but he looked thoughtful.

"We gonna find a way out."

That night was the most difficult for Tatiana. Not even when Rupert died was she so unsettled. She knew she had to do something about it, but she wasn't sure running away was the solution.

Next day she didn't go to school. She didn't go home either. She lived with Seth, planning their running away.

"On Tuesday we set off."

"It's a 3 day long trip by bus, Seth! Are you aware of that? Where will we get the money from?!"

"I got some cash from mom, but that won't be enough. We need more."

"My parents are broke. There is no way I could get any from them!"

"Leave it for now. We have one mo' week to solve that."

The next day Tatiana went to school, even if she wasn't planning to. She had a friend she could trust there, Marry, so she though that girl might be able to help her with some money.

"I'm so sorry, Tats, I ain't got nothing on me, and mom cut off my pocket cash for stealing from that shop."

"It's ok, Marry, thanks anyway."

"I hope you and Seth find a way out."

"Tatiana?" Their chat was interrupted by Mrs. Johnson, their head-teacher, an old and kind lady that had understanding for anyone. "Could you come with me for a second?"

"Of course, Mrs. Johnson" They left the class and went to the head-teacher's room.

"You've been absenting for a week now. What's the matter?"

"I…" she didn't know what to say.

"I know you live in a troubled family, but you have a brilliant future ahead, Tatiana. Don't waste it." Mrs. Johnson spoke with a warm parental voice, a voice Tatiana forgot what sounded like. "I will be back in a minute" The head-teacher left. Her purse was on the desktop. Tatiana started getting thoughts, what if she could grab some cash from there. She wouldn't notice anyway, and then, even if she did, Tatiana would be long gone. As she grabbed the purse and opened it, the door squeaked as Mrs. Johnson came in.

"Tatiana?"

"I… I'm so sorry, Mrs. Johnson.. I didn't mean to…" and she started crying. She was crying like a baby despite her being 19 years old.

"Oh, Tatiana. My heart is tearing to see you like this…"

"I am so sorry" she murmured through tears "I only wanted to…"

"What do you need the money for?" Tatiana hesitated to answer. "Come one, you can tell me."

"We are planning to run away…"

"With Seth…" the head-teachers mumbled, as she knew the two have been together for more than two years.

"Yes... but I swear I didn't mean to... We just need money..." and she continued crying in silence.

"Look... I didn't grow up in the best family either, and I feel you. I will give you 200 hundred dollars, that's all I got on me, but! You have to promise as soon as you settle down, you will go finish high school and go to college. And no one has to know about this. You hear me?" Tatiana was surprised.

"You hear me, Tatiana? Take this, they're yours." And she handed Tatiana the 200 bucks. The girl grabbed them sobbing and nodding her head.

"Thank you... Thank you, Mrs. Johnson, I promise I will."

When Tatiana got back to Seth, he was all jacked up about the 200 bucks. Their plan seemed perfect. They would leave on next Wednesday, as Seth decided, taking the bus from Lake St & 33rd Ave S. They would have to take 4 different buses, and make 6 main stops till Charleston. As they get there, David, Seth's friend, the one with the trailer, would meet them at the bus station. Tatiana gathered all the things she considered indispensable, and so did Seth. They were ready for the trip.

Chapter 2

"I'm glad we left." Tatiana whispered while laying her head on Seth's shoulder.

"What's the time?" he asked.

"Half past 6. We gonna be in sha-town in 'bout 2 hours."

"Good. I'm sick of this shitty bus."

"Well, maybe you should get down, young man." A raspy voice from behind said.

"The hell?" Seth turned around to see an old man all dressed up, with a black hat and a funky cane.

"I said…" and he maybe a long pause "…maybe you should get down if you don't like it in here."

Seth got visible angry. "You wan' me get down, honky?!"

"Seth…" Tatiana tried to calm him down.

"You what, honky?"

"Young man, you should calm down. Don't forget you're in public transportation. Get up and leave if you don't know how to behave around civilized people."

"Fuck you, cracka!"

"I see giving you rights served no good." The old white man insulted him while looking at his watch. Seth turned pale and jumped out of his seat and, before he got to hit the old man, another guy caught his hand and hold him tight.

"Let me off!! I wanna smack that cracka face!!"

Everyone in the bus panicked.

"Imma slit yo face, honkey!" Seth continued struggling.

"What's happening over there?" The driver stopped the bus, after seeing the danger of a fight starting.

"Well, we have a misbehaving young man over here." The old man smiled in ridicule pointing at Seth. All this time Tatiana was shaking scared on her seat. The driver looked pissed.

"I'm afraid you're gonna have to leave, sir."

"The fuck?! This honkey dissin' me here and I gotta leave?!" Seth was still angry.

"Sir…" the driver didn't give up.

"Let's go, Seth" Tatiana grabbed his arm shaking. Seth looked very mad, and he only gave in because he saw she looked scared.

"Imma rip that colorless shit head if I see him again." Seth mumbled while getting off of the bus.

"Great…" Tatiana was frustrated. "Now what we gonna do?"

"We gonna find a way, Tats, don't worry." Seth sounded reassuring.

They are a few miles past Madison when the bus driver forced them to get off. Tatiana was really scared, but she was thankful it was morning at least. Seth said they'd walk till the next bus station, after all, all they had was 2 bags of clothes and some snacks Tatiana grabbed in a hurry from a gas station, so walking some wouldn't hurt. They were in luck though, or so they thought. A blue van, heading towards their direction, passed by a few minutes later, and stopped. A young white boy opened the window and waved at them.

"Where are we heading, people?!" the guy seemed visibly dizzy.

"Charleston." Seth replied shortly.

"Woah! People! You got lucky today! My bros and I are heading right there! Come on in!"

His grin made Tatiana worry, so she whispered to Seth.

"Maybe we shan't go, Seth. I don't like 'em."

"Me neither, but we gotta get there somehow."

"So? Are you coming with us, man?!" the guy from the van asked. Seth and Tatiana agreed to go, they had no other choice, so they approached the van. The guy from the wheel got down and opened the van's back door. "Everybody get down! Now!" and he started laughing. Three other guys got down. They were all looking pretty high.

"I'm Johnathan." The skinniest guy presented himself and shook Seth's hand.

"I'm Seth, and this my girlfriend, Tatiana."

"Hi." She waved and smiled. The guy who's been driving introduced himself, too, as Jerry, he seemed the happiest guy in the world, but his grin was creepy as hell.

"This in Max, and this is Tom, they don't talk a lot." He pointed at the other two friends who didn't seem very pleased. Then he talked a bit about his trip to South Carolina, and how they got weed from a guy that works in a night club, and how they've escaped a cop, and lots of other nonsense that no one seemed eager to listen to. "Come on in!" He finally invited them to take a seat.

Seth and Tatiana got in, and after them climbed the first two guys, whose names neither Seth nor Tatiana remembered, and the skinny guy sat in front, next to Jerry, the one driving. A good 20 minutes of awkward silence followed.

"So!" Jerry, all of a sudden, interrupted the silence. "Why Charleston?"

"We got folks there." Seth didn't seem very eager to answer.

"Are you gonna live there?" Jerry insisted.

"We stayn' there for a while."

"I see. And where are you coming from? Why leaving?"

"Man, you wanna kno' too much."

"Seth…" Tatiana didn't want any trouble, so she replied for him "We wanna be alone, together, that's all."

"Lovebirds." The guy next to her said making a huge grin and poking her arm with his middle finger. She was getting annoyed but tried not to pay attention. Jerry kept staring at her and Seth through the mirror, from time to time, and silence sat upon them all once again. He was driving pretty fast, and at certain points Tatiana's knockers were shaking, and the guy who poked her kept staring like a creep the entire time. She felt very uncomfortable, but, there was nothing she could do about it. They were giving her and her boyfriend a ride, after all.

"You have a really hot girlfriend" the guy burst in the end.

"I don't think that's polite, Tom." Jerry said and started laughing.

"It really isn't." Tatiana replied, while Seth was getting pissed, but they were in the middle of nowhere, the road was deserted, so they had to, either endure, or get down and risk coming across some other even crazier white boys, so he kept silent.

"I don't think you mind though, being paid attention to and all." The guy next to her continued while poking her arm again, but this time, his finger didn't stop at the poke, but he ran it down her arm till her elbow. She grabbed her arm with her other hand and pulled herself closer to Seth. Seth noticed.

"Listen, man, thanks for da ride, but we should really get down." He tried to sounds as polite as possible "How much we owe you?"

"Did you hear that, Tom?" Jerry laughed looking at the guy next to Tatiana. He turned his head to the guy next to him.

"I don't know, maybe you tell us, Max?" the other guy laughed, too. The only silent one was the skinny one.

"Look, we don't have much on us, but we gonna give you everythin', just… stop." Tatiana sounded very worried.

"Calm down, Tats, it's all good." Seth tried to reassure her everything is fine, but he himself was worried.

"Yeah, you heard him, everything is going to be fine, Tats!" Jerry yelled laughing. Suddenly he stopped the van, and he was laughing no more. He opened the door, and the two guys got down.

"You stay in here." Jerry said to the skinny guy, who turned pale.

"Come on, get down, you pretty!" Tom laughed. Tatiana got off and so did Seth.

"Look, man, we don' have to get rough or somethin'." Seth said.

"Ha-ha! You heard that, Tom? We don' have to get rough or somethin'!" Jerry mocked Seth.

"Listen, man..." but he didn't get to finish as he was punched in his stomach by Max, the taller from the two.

"Seth!" Tatiana screamed while Tom, the other guy, grabbed her hands and hold her tight.

"Shut up, bitch!" Max yelled.

They kept beating Seth until he couldn't stand on his feet anymore. They checked his pockets and took all the money he had.

"You're lucky I don't fuck black bitches." Jerry spitted Tatiana in her face. Tom let her loose and she fell on her knees next to her unconscious boyfriend.

"Fuckin' white boy! That's why you never gonna gain our trust! You racist bastard!" Tatiana was in pain, she never saw Seth like this. The white boys got into their blue van and drove off, leaving them behind without any money. There were at least 10 more miles till Chicago, and there was no way on earth she could carry him all that way, besides that, they had the two backpacks. All she could do was lay there on her knees in despair. She tried waking him up, but that didn't work.

Finally, after at least an hour, another car approached them. It was an old grey jeep, and a black woman was driving. Tatiana got up and started waving at her to stop. The woman stopped, and got down.

"Holly Molly! What happened, girl?!" the black woman got off her jeep. "It was the crackers, right?"

All Tatiana could do was nod her head, while tears were falling down her cheeks.

"Where you headin'?"

"Charleston, but Sha-town would be great, to the bus station at least…"

"Get in, girl, lemme help you with that nigga, your boyfriend?"

"Yes."

The woman helped Tatiana get Seth in the car, on the backseat, and they sat together in the front. She told the young girl lots of interesting things about her life. She was currently going to visit her sister in Chicago, but she said she'd take them till Charleston.

"Listen, girl, I have a daughter myself, and if any nigga or cracka tryina hurt her, Imma slit some throats. I wan' no cracka mock ya and yo boyfriend, so Imma make sure you get to Charleston."

They got to Chicago in about 20 minutes, but the woman kept driving, she said she'd visit her sister on her way back. She really seemed to care, even if she had no idea what Tatiana's life story was. Soon Seth turned to life, and he was very surprised by the good deed the woman offered to do. They drove till evening, and then they stopped at a motel. When Tatiana told her they have no money left, the woman paid for everything and told them not to worry. It was the first time when the young unhappy girl experienced pure kindness from a stranger.

"Why you so kind to us?" Tatiana kept asking throughout the evening, puzzled. And the answer was always the same: "I know what's like to hav' to see white boys everyday knowin' they'd slit ya throat if they could."

It seemed like the woman had known what it's like to be hated for your race more than anyone else, and she was ready to help whoever in need.

Chapter 3

A trailer on Beaufain Street wasn't the best thing ever, but it was enough for now. There was a small bed, a tiny improvised kitchen, a small shower cabin, and even a living room kind of thing. It was actually way-way better than expected. The only problem was money.

"I'm starving…" Tatiana murmured.

"I feel ya… come'ere." He gave her a nice hug. "You know, I was thinkin', maybe there's a way to make some cash..."

"Yeah? Will yo hommie help us or somethin'?"

"Not really, Tats, but…" he hesitated.

"Wha'? Tell me, Seth."

"Ugh, you could do some… you know… some movement…"

"Seth? I don' get ya."

"They pay big dough for some night action…"

"You mean…"

"It's just for a night, Tats, we really need cash if we wanna survive…"

"You wouldn't fuckin' dare talk me into prostitution, Seth…" she got mad.

"Don' look at it like dat, Tats…"

"Don' ya fuckin' dare, Seth! I ain't no hoe! You hear me?!" she pulled away from Seth's embrace. "Do I look likea hoe, Seth? Do I? You think I came here to fuck rich niggas?! I could fuck rich niggas in my hometown, too, ya hear me?!"

"If it wasn't for me you'd still suck yo dad's dick!"

"Don' ya talk shit 'bout me, Seth! You know what a rough life I lived! I ain't gonna suck no dick fo' money! I ain't gonna do that! Ya hear me!?"

Seth kept yelling back at her, calling her the worst names that came to his mouth, until Tatiana started crying. It's then when Seth knew he messed up. He went to her and hugged her.

"I'm sorry, Tats... I didn't mean to... I love you, bu' we need some cash real' quick, so I thought..." She kept crying like she didn't hear a word, when suddenly she looked him in the eyes.

"Imma do it, if you wan' yo girl to suck dick for money, Imma do it."

"Tats, don' get me wrong…"

"Imma do it." And she was determined. Seth grabbed her tighter and kissed her neck while she kept sobbing. Truth is the thought of doing something like that scared her, but Seth's kisses could make wonders. He took off her shirt and kept kissing her.

"You always find a way to get yo hand in my drawers…" she whispered, and helped him take off her brown bra that matched her milk chocolate skin so perfectly well.

"An' you know you wan' it…" he whispered back as he slid his hand in her panties. "Imma punish you for bein' a bad… bad… girl…"

She moaned as he started fingering her pussy while playing his tongue on her neck. She arched her back asking for more, and he gave her more. He had her help him take his sweatpants off, and then his boxers. She started teasing him as she grabbed her dick and started gently stroking. She leaned to kiss him and then slowly lowered her head until she was close enough to place her lascivious tongue on his dick, preparing him for a blowjob. Seth grabbed her boobs and squeezed them so tight she moaned.

Next thing they were both naked and fucking like two wild animals on the small bed, just like it was their last time doing it.

Chapter 4

The first time is always tough, she figured. There she was standing, dressed like a hoe, you could see her booty cleavage, as well as her upper one. She never used make up in her life, she was naturally gorgeous, but tonight she put on a red lipstick she found in a purse under their trailer bed, probably from the previous owners, and her eyes were smoky. She tied her hair in a bun, as that always made her feel more confident.

Not very long after that, an expensive BMW, like she's never seen before stopped next to her. The driver's window lowered, and a bald black head showed up.

"You goin' anywhere tonight, sexy momma?"

"Are you takin' me anywhere?"

"Jump in."

She didn't wait for a second invite, she opened the door for herself and took a seat next to him. He drove into a dark alley and then told her to go on the backseat. She followed his order, and there she was, ready to do something she never thought she would. He got in.

"Don' make me regret droppin' money on ya." He said with his eyes pointing at his package. He spread his legs and Tatiana got on her knees in front of him. It wasn't the most comfortable position, but she needed the money. She placed her hands on his knees and started sliding her hands up to his cock. She made eye contact and the rich nigga was charmed by her looks, and he kept grinning. She unzipped his pants, pulled his cock out, and stuffed it in her mouth fake moaning. She kept making eye contact while sucking on it harder and harder. She noticed a ring on his finger and it had 'Samira' written on it, his wife probably. Lots of thoughts started tormenting her, and she felt like throwing up right there, but she had to go on.

"I wanna see dat pussy..." he said breathless. Tatiana pulled her short skirt up, and her panties aside, sliding his hard cock up her pussy.

"Momma, you so tight" he moaned as she rocked her body on him back and forth, back and forth. "Jump on me, momma, show me what you got." He continued, pulling down her tight top and squeezing her boobs so hard they turned pale. Tatiana made a jumping motion up and down on him, pleasing him more. In the end she felt the pleasure herself, forgetting about anything and anyone for a second.

She was there, in the moment, having sex for money with a stranger, but she felt good, so good it disgusted her.

An hour later she was again on the same street corner, but this time her make-up was ruined, and she had 400 bucks. The rich nigga was really generous, but only because she was gorgeous and she did a good job. Tatiana returned to the trailer, took Seth, and together, they went to the nearest minimarket to buy food. They also got alcohol, because Seth felt like it was something they needed to celebrate.

The next day Seth talked Tatiana into doing it again. And so a week has passed, and having a client each night started to become a habit, while Seth was slowly transforming into a more and more violent boyfriend, who acted more like a pimp.

"Tonight is the last time Imma do it. We got enough cash for a while now." She finally managed to say after seeing it's all getting out of hand.

"But Tats, don' ya see how well it's goin'? We could pay rent with dis dough you makin'!"

She didn't reply, but deep inside she decided this is the last time. She took the purse she bought 2 days ago and left. Wearing the same mini-skirt and tight top. She didn't have to wait long at the Lockwood Boulevard and Beaufain Stree intersection, in fact, she never had to wait long. A white guy wearing a leather jacket approached her. He was visibly under drugs.

"Hey, what's up?" he sounded very nervous. "How much do you want for the night, 'cause I'll pay you double, you coming?"

"Sure thing, bad boy." Tatiana smiled sounding real' confident.

He took her hand and started walking up the boulevard, until they reached Wentworth Street, and there was his car parked.

"We're going to my place, there you can do your job." He started the car, still very nervous, anxious almost. He drove up on Wentworth Street until the reached Grace Church Cathedral. There they got down. Tatiana was confused.

"We're almost there…"

"What, in the church?"

"Nah, I can't get in, but there's this annex we broke in."

"We?"

"Yeah, my friends and I." and he laughed anxiously.

"Wait, I don' think you got me right."

"No, no, he got you right, girl." Another voice came from inside the annex. Tatiana got scared, but she knew trying to run wouldn't have been any good, so she did what she was told to, and entered the annex. There were lots of church chairs and piles of books everywhere, religious books, as she figured. There were five guys, but she couldn't distinguish their facial features very well as it was relatively dark, the only light source was the moon breaking through a broken window pane.

"Common, girl, don't be shy." One of them said unzipping his pants.

"Maybe we should get her in the mood first!" another one suggested.

The third guy pulled out of his pocket of colorful small pills. She could see the colors because the guy opened the pack in the moonlight. He took two pills at once, and so did each guy.

"Common, don't be shy, girl, it'll make you feel free." A guy said calmly. At first he hesitated, but then she just took them and swallowed them fast. One of the guys started fondling her boobs through her tight top. She was braless and her visibly hard nipples were turning the guys on. Another guy grabbed her ass and squeezed it in both his hands. She kneeled down and started sucking on a cock. Soon there was another cock poking her face, and she had to alternate between the two. A third guy started finger her. The other two were both masturbating while squeezing her boobs. Very soon Tatiana started to get an euphoric sensation, something she's never felt before. All of a sudden everything felt several times better and more intense. A guy penetrated her and started bagging her aggressively, but she felt like it was the best thing ever. The guy previously fingering her offered Tatiana his cock too, so now she had to do the sucking on three guys. The euphoric feeling continued while the five guys were fucking her each the way he could. One of the guys stopped for a moment to give her two more pills, and she was totally into it. The frenzy continued for a long time during which all she mumbled was "Fuck, this feelz good…" from time to time. Soon she started feeling clumsy, her knees got weaker, her eyes started moving faster and she seemed to stop functioning as she blacked out several times.

It was around 5 am. Tatiana woke up on a pile of books all messy.

"The fuck…" She had no idea where she was. She looked around confused, and it soon became all clear. She remembered fucking the five guys, she remembered taking the pills, but she also remembered the euphoric feeling she got from them. She was so relaxed and carefree. For a moment everything she worried about, Seth's abuse, the trailer, her parents back home, everything literally disappeared. She had to get more of that. She had to, or so she thought. She wasn't dependent, but she liked it, and she found shelter from the real life in that.

Chapter 5

She was all alone on the street, heading up the Rutledge Ave, where she saw a strip club and lots of eerie guys who she supposed could sell Molly. She had 100 bucks on her, and no idea how much a dose would cost. She finally reached her destination. Unlike the other nights she was dressed decently. Seth had no idea where she was. Tatiana had her hair untied, and her face make-up free. She looked great, and everyone outside the strip club eyed her. She approached one of the guys who were looking like they'd sell somethin'.

"I wanna buy a dose o' Molly for my friend." She said anxiously. The guy knew she wasn't seeking a dose for her, in fact, he could swear she was sent there by police, though, if it was police, they wouldn't look for Molly, they'd look for more serious stuff, unless Molly was just an excuse.

"Sure… Sure" he replied measuring her head to toes. "Come with me."

She followed him, and they got inside the strip club through a 'stuff only' door. They walked through a relatively long corridor, then a room, and then they got in front of a wooden door.

"Gun Gun's no fool, girl." He said as he opened the door and pushed Tatiana in. She fell on her knees on the floor. It was a big room, with a desk and a leather chair. On the right side of the room was a couch, and there was sat a tall muscular guy. He was counting money.

"Who's this, Gun?" he asked without even looking.

"I think she might be a dog sent, boss..."

Gun Gun was Kedron's right hand, the guy on the couch. They have been knowing each other for a very long while now, and if there was anyone Kedron trusted, that was Gun.

"She???" Kedron raised his head and looked at the young beautiful girl kneeling on the floor still. "Who are you?"

"I'm Tatiana, I just…"

"She said she wants to buy a dose of Molly… for her friend."

"A dose of Molly?" a long pause followed "and that's it?"

"That's true." She said facing the ground.

"Then give her a dose of Molly, nigga. Actually, wait…" he stood up and gave Tatiana his hand to help her up. "Tatiana, you said?"

"Yes…" she hesitated.

"Gun Gun, you can leave." He made a gesture to the door.

"That's mah best hommie. You lucky it was him seein' you." Kedron turned to Tatiana "why'd a knockout like you need any type of drugs?"

"I… I… I should pro'lly go…" she heading towards the door.

"Wait, mah name's Kedron. You seem a nice girl." His voice sounded genuine. Tatiana was rather scared and worried.

"It's OK, you can trust me." Then he turned to the guy who brought her there "You leave, nigga." The guy left. Kedron invited Tatiana to sit on the couch. "I ain't gonna hurt you." The girl sat on the couch and Kedron sat on a chair next to the couch, keeping a decent distance. He asked Tatiana to tell him about her, and was moved when she told him her life story. They talked a lot, and she seemed to trust him more than she has ever trusted anyone else, even if it was the first time she saw him. There was something about him. The way he moved his hands while talking, his expressions, and his genuine concern made her feel nice. In the end he gave her a dose of Molly for free.

"Imma give it to you for 30 bucks only, cuz you're a cute girl."

"Thank you."

"You can come here whenever you want, just tell the nigga you saw earlier Kedron is waitin' for ya."

Tatiana thanked him a few more times before she left. She went straight 'home', the poor trailer she and Seth still lived in.

"Where have you been?" Seth asked with a suspicious face as soon as she got in.

"I was in downtown, waiting for some client, but no one came."

"Why you lyin'? Huh?" he got close to her and touched her jawline in disgust.

"I ain't lyin', Seth."

He tried to kiss her, but she protested.

"Oh, so there's someone…" he turned around.

"There ain't no one, I just… can't tonight."

"Wha? You gonna tell me you on yo fuckin' period?"

"In fact I am." And she wasn't lying. Seth didn't care, she grabbed her and dragged her to bed. She tried opposing him, but he was stronger. He grabbed her with his right hand by the throat and begun strangling her.

"Seth! Let me go!" she punched him. Seth didn't let go, instead he slid his left hand in her panties.

"You on yo fuckin' period, bitch, right?! How you like that?! Huh?!"

Poor Tatiana kept trying to free herself, but it was in vain. Seth pulled his hand out and his fingers were covered in her blood. He smeared them on her face and then grabbed her throat with both hands and begun strangling harder. Tatiana got even more panicked, her face was turning red. She was frantically punching him until she griped on a china vase from the small nightstand, next to the bed, and smacked it on Seth's head. He shook his head in confusion as he did not see that coming, while Tatiana took the chance to escape. She run out barefooted and kept running a few blocks until she felt safe. Tatiana stopped in a dark alley and cuddled next to a trash can. Realizing she still has the Molly dose on her she took the two pills and swallowed them quickly. Minutes later she was lying on the ground feeling euphoric, while the view itself was horrible. A barefoot girl, with her face covered in blood, lying on the cold ground with a creepy grin on her face.

Chapter 6

Days were passing by, things were getting worse between Tatiana and Seth, more fights, more sexual abuse, she felt worse than ever. Molly was her only way of escaping this terrible thing she was calling 'life'. She begun giving blowjobs in an effort to make money for drugs. No night was passing without her taking up to five pills of happiness.

It was late night. Tatiana went to Kedron for Molly, as usually. He knew she'd come so he was waiting for her. As she got in he made her a coffee.

"Common, Kedron, you know why I'm here, I'm hurryin'."

"Take a seat first, I wanna talk."

She sat down and drunk the coffee, even if her thought were on Molly non-stop already.

"I really like you." He said all of a sudden. Tatiana, being attracted to him herself, lightened. "And I mean it, like… ain't no girl there makin' me feel like dis."

She quickly gave him a shy kiss on his lips, and he froze. He was sitting there completely frozen. It was simply so unexpected, and pleasant, and sudden. He had no words. All he could think of was pull her up to his chest and pet her head. It was rather a reflex than a pre-planned action.

"I don' wanna return to Seth." She whispered and a tear rolled down her cheek.

"You can sleep here on the couch tonight. It ain't very comfy but it's safe."

"Thank you, Kedron." She murmured. Kedron said he'd be writing papers all night, so she doesn't have to worry about anything. Writing papers? That sounded more like an excuse to watch her during the night, but it was one hundred times better than sleeping next to an abusive boyfriend. An hour later she was already sleeping. Kedron went out for a few minutes and told Gun Gun about this girl sleeping there for the night. He didn't want anyone disturbing him with any kind of business. When he got back he sat in his leather chair, made himself some coffee and kept admiring her curves. He really liked this girl, he never liked someone as much as to really care.

Must have been around 4 am when Tatiana woke up. She started shivering as she was cold.

"You OK?" Kedron asked. She mumbled something back, but all he understood was 'cold'. He stood up and sat on the couch next to her. He wanted to touch her face, but hesitated. The sleepy girl cuddled up to him, he was strongly moved by the gesture. He laid next to her and kissed her forehead. She said some gibberish, and he smiled. For some reason just seeing her sleeping turned him on. In the end he couldn't help it, so he kissed her on her lips. She woke up, but instead of panicking or something, she kissed him back, and she continued kissing and touching him.

They ended up having sex. Quality sex.

"I never felt like this before..." she whispered after they finished.

"I hadn't either." And he kissed her once more on her forehead.

She never felt better, and she knew she can't let go, unfortunately for her,

Seth wasn't going to give up on her easily.

"Do you have any Mollies in here?" she finally asked.

"Tatiana…" Kedron replied "you better give up on those, they may seem harmless, but they can kill ya."

"Kedron… I know wha' I'm doin'."

Kedron however knew from his own experience that drugs, no matter what kind, bring trouble, big trouble, terrible trouble, and she needed to get rid of the habit until it wasn't too late. He decided to do his best to pursue the girl he liked into quitting, so the next morning he told her he's not going to give her any Mollies, and he also let her know how much he cared about her. Tatiana listened, but didn't take the quitting thing really seriously. She took it more as Kedron being bossy with her, since he was 2 years older than her, besides, as she figured later, he was member of the Chuck Town Trey~ Deucez, an offshoot of the infamous Piru Bloodz street gang, and that definitely gave him a lot of authority. Little did she know about Kedron's life before he became a drug dealer though. She was curious, but she didn't have the guts to ask yet.

She went back to Seth. She was visibly colder, and Seth was getting rougher with her, yelling at her every second. He also found out about her

Molly habit, and when she told him she wants to quit, he just laughed at her, and tried putting her down by telling her how she's a failure, and how she's never gonna get to do anything with her life. He even swore that she's gonna become a drug addict, and suck dick for the rest of her life, in order to get a gram of something. His behavior was tearing her apart, she definitely couldn't tolerate it anymore, but there was nothing she could do about it, not now, at least. She had to keep strong. She knew better times are coming, but she had to keep strong now, she wanted to prove Kedron she knows what she's doing, and she can stop using Mollies without him pursuing her to do so. All she could think of now was proving Kedron she's worth it all. She wanted to show him she's not like everyone else, she knew she's stronger and she can do better than that. If there was anyone Tatiana wanted ever to impress, this was him, this was the right person. She was growing affectionate of Kedron, and she didn't want to let that feeling go. This girl was ready to go against her every habit in order to gain Kedron's trust, and he kinda knew it, he kinda realized that, but he didn't want to jumpt to conclusions too fast, he was a very calculated man, even when it came to feelings, that might even have been his weakness.

Chapter 7

"Tell me about yo past, Kedron…"

"You wanna know about my past? I ain't sure you ready for dat, Tatiana…"

"I trust ya… you can trust me, too."

"I had a tough childhood… the one I called 'father' was a faggot. He beat mom to death one night, and then the nightmares begun…"

Tatiana hugged him. He continued speaking with a kind of indifference, remembering the rough times. "He got a boyfriend right after mom's funeral. She was such a kind lady… Fo' 5 years I been molested by that faggot's bitch, a nigga twice his age… I was 6…"

Although it was Kedron's life story, Tatiana was the one crying. He, on the other hand, seemed cold to the past. He knew he couldn't change anything.

"I started working in a restauran' as a dishwasher at 15. There I met Gun Gun. No one knows his real name, not even him. The restauran' was Big Guy's place. Three years aftah he took me in, he said I was robust, an' he needed guys like me. Then I talked him into takin' Gun Gun in, too."

Big Guy was one of the main heads of Deucez, and he was the one who gave all the authority Kedron had. He basically became like a father since he took Kedron in.

"I, myself, had drug trouble, serious trouble, that's why I'm tellin' ya to quit Mollies now, when you still can."

"I will, I promise I will."

"When will you stop seein' that nigga?"

"I need to let 'im know about you…"

And there she was again, in the trailer, fighting with Seth.

"Imma leave you if you keep abusing me, Seth, I'm sick an' tired of yo games." She finally told him.

"You what? Ha-ha! An' whatchu gonna do 'bout it?! Run to that nigga you keep seein'? You though I wouldn't find?!"

"I don' care, but Imma leave ya if you keep doin' this!"

"Oh, someone didn't take her pill tonight!"

"I'm takin' pills no mo'."

"Sure thing! Bitch! Here!" and he pulled out of his pocket a hand of pills that he'd been gathering specifically for this moment. He threw the pills in her face yelling and telling her how's she's worth nothing. Tatiana begun crying. "Common! Gather dem and eat them, fuckin' cunt! You worth nothin' more than a Molly pill! Take 'em! Take 'em to escape yo fuckin' worthless shit reality!"

And she did so, she threw four pills at once down her throat. She was desperate, she just wanted to feel calm for a second. Somehow, she was at her weakest when around Seth. If there was someone who could destroy her, that was definitely Seth. All kind of thoughts started flooding her mind, she felt weak, for some reason the pills seemed to not work anymore, she found two more Mollies on the floor and swallowed them, too.

"Molly ain't the only thing you swallowin' tonight, bitch!" he yelled unzipping his pants "On yo knees, bitch!"

Tatiana tried to run, but he caught her by her hand and pushed her down on the floor. "You either suckin' or getting' punched, bitch!" he sounded angrier than ever. She got scared, so she did and he told her. She starting sucking on his dick while being disgusted by the situation she got herself in once again. Why did she even return if she knew what's waiting for her? That not even her could answer. If Kedron saw her right now, he'd smack Seth's face, and she knew it, but the thing was Kedron had no idea she had to go through this kind of abuse. If only he knew, if only he saw her now, but he couldn't see her… if only…

Tatiana passed out, she had taken an overdose, she's never taken so many pills at once. Taking advantage of her being blacked out, Seth raped her, and then left her on the floor.

"Ya deserve that, bitch."

She woke up in the middle of the night shaking because of the Molly, this tie she didn't even remember having the euphoric feeling, everything was numb, all she remembered was Seth aggressively yelling and throwing the pills at her. Her feet were ice cold, and so were her hands. It was too far for her to go to Kedron, but she needed rest and heat, so she had no choice. She laid in bed, silently crying and regretting leaving home. She was abused there. Called names and hated, by her own family, but she had Mary, her friend, and Mrs. Johnson, the kind head teacher. She also had the cheerleading team, and hopes for the future. Even Seth was a good guy back then. But, on the other hand, here, in Charleston, she met Kedron, and right now, he was the only thing keeping her alive.

Chapter 8

Tatiana decides she won't see Kedron until she lives at least a week without Molly, but she thought he deserves to know. She went to the strip club where he always was, and approached Gun Gun.

"You wanna see Kedron?"

"No, not tonight, but I wan' ya to tell him somethin'."

"Sure, whatevah ya say, girl."

"Tell him I will see him only next week, and tell 'im not to look after me. Imma stay safe, just getting' over the habit. I ain't gonna come here and he better not come there."

"I don' think boss will be happy to hear that."

"You tell 'im that, if he cares he'll listen."

She left, while Gun gun went straight to Kedron's office.

"Boss, we gotta talk."

"What's up, homie?"

"Yo girl came."

"Didn' I say let her in whenever?"

"Yeah, but it ain't that, she said she ain't gonna come here for a week."

"Wha'? Did she say why?"

"She wanna get over the habit. So she said."

"Aha, I see… you can go, Gun, thanks, man…" Kedron was cofused, he didn't know wether to worry or trust Tatiana. He decided to do the latter.

Tatiana said she won't leave the trailer until she's sure she's clean, and although Seth kept yelling and threatening her, she just did it her way.

"You changed a lot since we got here, Seth…"

"You changed too…" It was one of the rare times, when Seth was actually sober and calm.

"I mean, you actually cared back there, when I was with mah folks. I'd never thought you'd become my pimp…"

"I ain't no pimp, Tats, we needed that cash, an' you kno' it better."

"I was your girlfriend, Seth…" she sounded really disappointed.

"Was? You mean…"

"I don' know, I don' see no future for us…"

He didn't say anything. Perhaps because he was clear minded. He got up and left, but Tatiana knew he would be sober no more in the evening, so she got up and hugged him like it was the last time she saw him. And, in a way, it was the last time, the last time she saw the Seth she's known for more than two years. The week, was coming to an end. Tatiana was more or less clean, and, strangely enough, Seth seemed to become a better man, or so it seemed, at least.

It was Saturday morning. Seth got ready to leave.

"I gotta see Nick, will you still be here tonight?"

"Yes." she replied shortly. He left. During the day, she cleaned the trailer one last time, for she planned to leave for good on Sunday morning. She was ready to even get back to Minneapolis in case things didn't work out with Kedron, so she got that, but one thing was sure, she was definitely not planning to stay here with Seth.

The night came. For some reason Tatiana had a really bad feeling. Not long after her bad feeling she heard voices outside. She could distinguish Seth's voice, but there were at least two more voices. The door of the trailer opened.

"Heyyyy, giiirl!" Seth was drunk.

"Hi, Seth."

"Heeeere, mah homie, Niiiick! And mah homie Jooooohn, and mah homie, nigga? I forgot yo nigga ass name!" and he burst into laughter. They all laughed, and they were all drunk. Tatiana got her jacket on and purse and wanted to leave.

"Uh-uh-uh, girlll! You ain't leaviiiin'… We gonna have some fun first, ain't that right, niggas?!" he looked at his three friends laughing.

"Seth, you are drunk, let me go…" but Seth would obviously not let her go.

"Show mah homies what you can do with that tooongue!" he yelled showing his tongue mimicking a tongue kiss. His friends laughed again. "Commong, niggas, wha' yo asses waitin' for? Come fuck mah bitch!"

"If you askin'." One of them said trying to grab Tatiana.

"Don't touch me, you son of a bitch!" she protested.

"Oh, we got a bad momma over 'ere!" another one exclaimed grabbing her boob. She was literally disgusted.

"Hold her for me first..." the third guy said. Seth and his friend Nick caught her by her arms and hold her tight, while the friend Seth didn't get to call by his name proceeded to rape her. Tatiana was screaming in tears and struggling to free herself, but it was in vain as they were stronger than her, and she was just a girl, after all. They all took turns to rape her and then cum on her face and hair. After that, Seth himself took a bottle of whiskey he brought along when he came with his friends and smacked it against Tatiana's half-conscious face. Her eye turned blue on the spot. Then he proceeded to take her on kicks calling her a slut and repeating several times that she's just an air waste. Two of his friends joined in kicking her with their feet, while the third one passed out.

"Fuck you, fuckin' bitch! You deserve it! You fuckin' waste!" Seth kept repeating all along, while Tatiana was laying unconscious on the floor.

He took her by the feet and another guy grabbed her by her hands, and together they took her out and threw her in the trash dumpsters.

"Die, bitch!" Seth furiously kicked the trash dumpsters one last time. Tatiana looked dead. The blue spots on her body were so visible on her now pale body. She was naked, and the night cold was hurting her even more. She was still lucky though. On the other side of the trash dumpsters, a homeless 50 year old man made bed. He saw what happened and took note of Seth and the other guy's facial features. The homeless man waited for them to leave and then quickly ran to Tatiana. He was scared to see such a beautiful young woman in a state like that. He dragged her down and then, taking her in his arms, he took her to his improvised bed behind the trash dumpsters. He covered her with some old rags he had and light a fire in a metal trash can he used as a fireplace. That was the best he could do for now, but that was enough to keep her alive. He tried waking her up, to ask her if she has any safe pace where he could take her, but she wasn't making a sound. The man put his ear next to her nose to hear if she's still breathing, and she was. He started shaking her gently until she started mumbling something.

"What is your name, lady? Where can I take you?"

"K…Ke-dron…"

"Kedron? Is that your name? IS that a trust person? Speak to me, lady!"

"Kedron… the strip club…"

"Where's that, lady? I'll take you there!"

"Rutledge… Ave…" she managed to say through violent coughs.

"Damn, that's far…" after a moment of thinking, the man continued "And your name, lady?"

"Tah…tee…ahna…"

"Stay here, lady, don't move, I will bring Kedron from the strip club here! I will be back as soon as possible, OK?!" he put one more cover on her and threw some more plastic in the metal trash can. It took the homeless man about half an hour to get to the strip club. He approached the guards that eyed him right away.

"I came here to talk to Kedron! Fast! His lady is hurt!"

The guards laughed at him and told him to vanish while he kept insisting Tatiana needs help. Due to the uproar Gun Gun, who was leaning towards a wall, approached them.

"What's happening here, niggas? Who dis cracka?"

"He wanna talk to Kedron ha-ha!" on of the guards exclaimed.

"But his lady is in trouble, Tatiana! She told me to come here and tell Kedron! You have to believe me!"

"What?!" Gun Gun was surprised to hear that. "You wait here." He said as he threw his cigarette on the ground. He run quickly inside, still through the 'stuff only' door. As soon as Kedron heard that, he ran out to talk to the white homeless himself.

"Wha' you sayin', man?"

"I need to talk to Kedron! That lady is going to die!"

"You talkin' to him right now. Where is she!"

"You need to come with me! You need to come with now! The lady is naked in cold!"

Kedron didn't need to hear more. He jumped in his car, took Gun Gun and the homeless man with him, and set off. He drove like crazy and in less than 5 minutes they was there. A few steps from the trailer, right next to the trash dumpsters. When Kedron saw the girl he cared about in that state he got all angry and determined.

"Those modafuckers are gonna pay with their own blood for this! Who did this to you, Tatiana, who did this to you?!"

"I saw them! They were two!" the homeless man shouted.

Kedron took Tatiana on his arms and hurried to his car.

"You're coming with us, man!" he pointed at the homeless. The man didn't protest. Kedron drove to his apartment. It was the first time he took Tatiana there, but this was sure not the way he imagined it'd be. As they got in, he told the homeless man and Gun Gun to make themselves comfy while he took Tatiana to his room and laid her on his bed, covering her with multiple sheets. He then made a call. In about 30 minutes another car arrived there. It was the guy Kedron called.

"Mah homie, so glad you here! She's in the bedroom!" Kedron showed him the way. "Please tell me she gonna be fine…" he was desperate. The doctor, who was in fact one of Kedron's cousins said he'd let him know soon. Kedron used the waiting time to ask the homeless man about the bastards who did that to Tatiana.

"Who are you?"

"My name is Jeremiah. I live where you saw your lady laying. I don't have a home."

"OK, Jeremiah, thank you for informing me about Tatiana, I won' be indifferent towards that. Now who were the motherfuckers who did that...?" Kedron was trying hard to keep his calm.

"They were two. The first one's name was Seth, I heard the other one telling him to go. The second one was his friend, but I didn't hear his name."

"Seth…motherfucker…" Kedron was burning with rage. "I fuckin' knew it… Imma slit that nigga's throat when I see 'im…"

The doctor opened the door making a gesture for Kedron to come.

"She's been raped multiple times, and then beaten. She's also got a broken leg, she needs a gypsum there. She's been brutally beaten, Kedron, but she's gonna survive, that I know."

Kedron was too mad to make a sound. He just nodded. The doctor continued "She's not under any drugs, nor alcohol, so I made her an injection so she can sleep without pain for the next few hours. I'll be back in about an hour with the gypsum."

"Thank you, man, those motherfuckers are gonna pay for dis."

He walked the doctor through the door. All this time Gun Gun got to find out more about Jeremiah, who once had a family and a job, but, after losing everything to gambling, he became a better man, homeless though. Kedron promised him a room in the building where the strip club was located. He told him he can live there for the rest of his life, if he wants, and he also gave him a job, and this job was to spy on Seth and find out who was the other guy, as neither Kedron, nor Jeremiah knew they were actually four, including Seth.

Chapter 9

It was around noon, and Jeremiah brought news "I got his name, Nick Jumbo." and that was all Kedron, really, wanted to hear.

"Nick fuckin' Jumbo!? That fuckin' motherfucker?! Imma rip his head off!"

"Do you know him? Do you know why he beat your lady?"

"Yes, I know that bastard, and I also know what he gonna get for that." Kedron called Gun Gun. He also told Jeremiah to watch Tatiana until he returns, and he left. He met with Gun Gun right on Beaufain Street, a few blocks away from Seth's trailer. Soon enough they were inside.

"Who are you, niggas? What you lookin' for here?!"

Kedron felt the urge to punch him in the face right there, but he had to resist, he wanted to find about the other guy to. Little did her know Tatiana was actually raped and beaten by four.

"I'm here to clear some things. Tatiana, where is she?" Kedron pretended to know nothing.

"Hah! That bitch!" Seth figured this was the guy Tatiana kept seeing. "Well, we... played a bit... and then she run..." he tried to sound as natural as possible, because Kedron was intimidating him, and he was afraid of a confronting with him.

"Fun, you say? Wha' kinda fun?"

"Me an' mah hommies, she asked for it!" and he became nervous. "She was fuckin' you, right?! That bitch!"

"You an' yo' hommies?!"

"Yeah, we were four, and she reaaally liked it in her ass, ha-ha!" Seth lost control, and he also ignored the fact that Kedron was a tall and muscular guy.

"Call 'em all here, now…" Kedron sounded very calm, but he also pointed a gun at him.

"Ho-ho-hold up, man! I was…foolin' around… She mah girlfriend, wouldn't hurt her!"

"Call 'em here, now, I said!" and he punched him hard in the face. Gun Gun was looking through the window, while Jeremiah kept shaking his head at the thought of what Seth did to his own girlfriend.

"You should do what he is telling you, young man."

"Shut da fuck up, cracka! Why you bringin' colorless shit here in mah house!?"

"Yo house? Mo' like a fuckin' trailer. Call Nick… Jumbo…."

"How you know his name?" Seth was surprised, few people knew that.

"I just know stuff… Call them now or Imma fuckin' shoot yo ass, nigga…" Kedron kept his cool. Seth didn't take him seriously, so he was not planning to call. However, Kedron was definitely joking, he pulled the trigger in Seth's right foot.

"You modafucker!!" he yelled in pain.

"Shhh, call yo niggas here, an' you better not scare them off. Tell them you got some benjamins and throwin' a party."

"Throwin' a party, ha-ha, look at 'im, boss!" Gun Gun laughed. Seth kept screaming, and when Kedron threatened to shoot him in the left foot, too, he grabbed the phone. After a few rings someone picked up the phone.

"Yo, nigga!" Seth tried to sound natural. "Come 'ere, homie, we throwin' a party!" A pause followed. "Yeah, yeah, bring John an' Rony along too, we gonna have… fun." This time he didn't sound really convincing, but his friends bought it, and, about an hour later, they were at Seth's place. In the meantime, Kedron had Seth tide on a chair, and gave him a few punches.

"Nigga? You here?!" one of the three guys outside shouted. Kedron put the gun at Seth's temple and told him to invite them in. He did as he was told. The guys got in without any further questioning, and as the first one got in Gun Gun grabbed him by the neck and knocked him down. Kedron pointed the gun at the other two and ordered them to come in and do as he says.

"Hold up, nigga, we owe you benjamins!?"

"No, yo asses owe me yo worthless lives." Kedron calmly replied, then he turned to Jeremiah "Thanks for yo help, man, we gonna get back to you soon." The kind man left because he sure did not want to see anything of what was going to happen next.

"Imma go straight to the subject, you niggas tell me every damn thing you did to Tatiana and Imma kill you fast." The calmness in his voice freaked everyone out. They knew he was determined and there was no escape.

"Man, we were drunk an' shit…" one of the starting whining.

"Aww, lil' nigga gonna cry???" Kedron tried impersonating. The guy continued.

"We only… had sex with her… an' then Seth thought it'd be cool to beat her up…"

"Oh, so it was Seth still… Seth, Seth, Seth, why ain't you a good boy? Huh? You know you gonn' pay, right?"

"He means it." Gun Gun said nodding.

They knew they fucked up, but this wasn't even the worst. Kedron shoot everyone in their feet, because why not? He wanted vengeance for Tatiana, and he wanted it in to happen in the worse way possible. The four guys were now all tied, with their feet covered in blood.

"You can leave, too, Gun Gun." Kedron shortly said, and Gun Gun left. As soon as he got out of the trailer's door, Kedron addressed to Seth.

"Show me yo' palms."

"Or wha'? You gonn' shoot me?"

"Yeah, an' this gonna teach you not to touch Tatiana again. That, if I leave you alive, which I highly doubt." And he shot him. He then turned to the next tied guy. "Yo hands?" But he didn't want to show his hands, shaking his head in fear, as he saw what happened to Seth.

"Just let me go… I ain't gonna tell no one, and never gonna touch anyone again…" he begged, but Kedron had no mercy, not now, at least.

"Oh, cool,we cool, man, we cool."
Kedron seemed to sympathize.

"Really?! Thanks, ma-" but he didn't
get to finish his quote as Kedron shoot
him right between his eyes. The other
two guys begged to be killed rather
than have their hands shot, like Seth
did, but Seth had another thing in
mind. He simply smiled at them
saying everything's gonna be fine,
and shot them in their balls. The
trailer sounded like a purgatory from
outside. The three guys left alive,
including Seth were screaming in
pain. Next thing Kedron did was
shoot Seth in his balls. He then went
out, took a tank of gasoline from his
car, and spread it all over the trailer.

He then lit a match and threw it, setting the trailer on fire, with the screaming rapists inside still.

Not long after, Kedron's phone rang. It was Big Guy, Piru Bloodz boss heard about the trailer thing. Kedron wouldn't expect him to be mad, and in fact, he wasn't. All he wanted was to tell Kedron how proud he is. It was surprising, as Kedron told him previously about this girl he cared for, and Big Guy said it's not very smart to risk his life for a bitch, but then again, he didn't know her story. That phone call really meant a lot to Kedron, as Big Guy was the one he respected more than anyone.

Chapter 10

It was morning, and Tatiana was still sleeping. Kedron went in the shower to wash off the criminal blood off of him. As he wanted to leave the shower, Tatiana got in, and hugged him from behind kissing his shoulder. He turned around and begun kissing her lips while squeezing her boobs. He never felt happier than this. He finally had the girl he loved safe, and she was all his. He grabbed her leg and pulled it up his hip as he gentle pushed into her. Tatian grabbed his back and pushed against him more.

The shower water falling down her spine and boobs only turned Kedron on more. While banging her, he passionately kissed her neck like he couldn't get enough of it. Tatiana was arching her back of pleasure, moaning as Kedron dived deeper into her.

"Ah, Kedron... You're killin' me with yo' passionate luv..." she was feeling the euphoric again, but this time it was pure love and passion, it was Kedron making her feel that way. He pushed her against the shower wall, and fucked her faster, and faster, until her legs started shaking, and her moans got louder, and louder.

"God, Kedron!" she shouted his name as her back arched in elation once again. He finished by nibbling on her neck and telling her how much he loves her, and how glad he is they were finally together. He took her to bed on his arms, and then he sat there next to her, making sure she feels loved, because she sure was loved. He hugged her, and reassured her she is now safe, and nothing bad is going to happen to her as long as he is alive.

"I really luv ya, Kedron..." she whispered.

"I luv you mo'." He smiled and gave her a kiss. "I should order some pizza, I'm starviiiiin'!" and he made a silly face at her. Hard to imagine a tough guy like him acting all sweet, but he really cared about her, so whatever made her happy was now his priority.

The pizza guy arrived relatively fast. Tatiana never ate so much in her entire life, while Kedron mostly looked at her eating, because she was so cute. Not only cute, she was gorgeous, the only knockout girl Kedron has even ever fell for.

"I ain't gonna let you go evah..." he said looking her in the eyes.

"You can't get rid of me that easy!" she giggled, and hugged him once more. They were both living in the moment, but they also had big plans for the future, for it was only the beginning...

CPSIA information can be obtained
at www.ICGtesting.com
Printed in the USA
LVOW04s1551090316
478459LV00016B/552/P